Hi, I'm Carrie

And David

Welcome to our **JUMP UP** and **JOIN IN** series.

We hope you enjoy reading the books and joining in with the songs.

This book is called **Elephant's Birthday Bells**.

It's all about **loud** and **soft**. It's lots of fun.

Yes it's very funny. Remember to **turn the page** when you hear this sound . . .

AROO!

EGMONT

We bring stories to life

First published in Great Britain 2013
by Egmont UK Limited,
The Yellow Building, 1 Nicholas Road, London W11 4AN
www.egmont.co.uk

Text copyright © Carrie and David Grant 2013
Illustrations copyright © Ailie Busby 2013

Carrie and David Grant and Ailie Busby have asserted their moral rights

ISBN 978 1 4052 5834 0

A CIP catalogue record for this title is available from the British Library

Stay safe online.
Egmont is not responsible for content hosted by third parties.

Please note:
Adult supervision is recommended when scissors are in use.

For our beautiful children
– who teach us all about being LOUD!
– Carrie and David –

For Panda,
the best cake baker ever. x
– Ailie –

EGMONT LUCKY COIN

Our story began over a century ago, when seventeen-year-old Egmont Harald Petersen found a coin in the street.

He was on his way to buy a flyswatter, a small hand-operated printing machine that he then set up in his tiny apartment.

The coin brought him such good luck that today Egmont has offices in over 30 countries around the world. And that lucky coin is still kept at the company's head offices in Denmark.

Carrie and David Grant

Elephant's Birthday Bells

Illustrations by Ailie Busby

Remember to turn the page when the elephant **aroos!**

EGMONT

Elephant's trumpeting was far too **loud** for the family band.

And her stomping and stamping was even noisier.

STOMP

STAMP!

So Mum and Dad
went to the music shop.

"We need to find an instrument to help Elephant play *quietly*," said Mum. "And a guitar is definitely not right!"

A few days later it was
Elephant's birthday.
"What could this jangly
present be?" she wondered.

It was some special Birthday Bells!

"The secret to playing them *quietly* is to be as graceful as you can," Mum said.

Elephant put the bells around her ankles and began to practise.

She *tiptoed* . . .

and teetered...

and tottered...

and **tripped!**

But Elephant didn't give up.

She practised and practised until she could walk *quietly* on her toes and the bells jingle-jangled beautifully.

She was a quiet and
graceful elephant.

The family band
sounded even better
with Elephant's new
jingly-jangly bells.

"I love my Birthday Bells," said Elephant happily.

Play

Chorus:
Ella, ella, ella, Elephant
Ella, ella, ella, Elephant
Ella, ella, ella, Elephant
Play something, play.

Get your bells on.
Not too hard, not too soft.
Get your bells on.
Not too fast, not too slow.
Get your bells on.
Not too loud, not too quiet.
Get your bells on.
Are you ready to go?

Get your bells on.
Not too hard, not too soft.
Get your bells on.
Not too fast, not too slow.
Get your bells on.
Not too loud, not too quiet.
Get your bells on.
Are you ready to go?

Happy Birthday to you!
Happy Birthday to you!

Chorus:
Ella, ella, ella, Elephant
Ella, ella, ella, Elephant
Ella, ella, ella, Elephant
Play something, play something.
Ella, ella, ella, Elephant
Ella, ella, ella, Elephant
Ella, ella, ella, Elephant
Play something, play something, play.

Get your bells on.
Not too big, not too small.
Get your bells on.
Not too high, not too low.
Get your bells on.
Not too sharp, not too flat.
Get your bells on.
Are you ready to go?

Get your bells on.
Not too big, not too small.
Get your bells on.
Not too high, not too low.
Get your bells on.
Not too sharp, not too flat.
Get your bells on.
Are you ready to go?

Happy Birthday to you!
Happy Birthday to you!

Chorus:
Ella, ella, ella, Elephant
Ella, ella, ella, Elephant
Ella, ella, ella, Elephant
Play something, play something.
Ella, ella, ella, Elephant
Ella, ella, ella, Elephant
Ella, ella, ella, Elephant
Play something, play something, play.

Play something, play.
Get your bells on.
Get your bells on.
Play.
Get your bells on.
Play something,
Play something, play.

Happy Birthday to you!
Happy Birthday to you!

When you play Track **7**, the karaoke track, sing along
to the whole song! Your special solo parts are in **bold**.

Sing Loud and Proud and Super Soft!

This story was all about **loud** and **soft**.

Learning how to sing or play
loudly and **softly** is lots of fun.

With your hands on a table (or drum)
tap out and count from one to four
over and over, like this:

1 2 3 4 1 2 3 4

Now whisper and tap softly.

1 2 3 4 1 2 3 4

Now try it a bit **louder**. . .

1 2 3 4 1 2 3 4

and now **very loudly**.
(Making sure you don't shout though!)

1 2 3 4 1 2 3 4

If there are two of you, one can call
soft, **medium** and **loud,** and the other
can try to get the commands right.

For our **Jump Up and Join In** series we really want to get children interested in music and how it works. It shouldn't have to be rocket science and we want to encourage you as a parent, teacher or carer to teach your children with confidence. If **you** can learn it then **you** can pass it on.

Track 6 **Heavenly Harmonies on the Stairs**

So in this book we're going to be moving on to singing in **harmony**. Look at the picture of the stairs. Let's think about our voice climbing the stairs and counting . . .

Now one person should sing and stay holding the note on the first step, number **one**.

The other person should count and sing from **one** to **three** and then hold the note on **three**.

Once you've got that you can even try climbing the stairs holding the **odd** numbers up to **seven**, like this:

o . . . . n . . . . . . e

one, two, t . . h . . r . . e . . e

one, two, three, four, f . . i . . v . . e

one, two, three, four, five, six, s . e . v . e . n

Make your own
Jingle-Jangle Bells!

You'll need:

Carboard tube (from inside a toilet roll or kitchen paper roll)
Bells (from old Christmas decorations or your local bead shop)
Pencil   Scissors   Glue   Different coloured ribbons
Needle and quite thick thread

Ask a grown-up to help you!

Step 1 Use your pencil to draw four dots at one end of your cardboard roll. Then repeat until you have gone round the whole roll.

Carefully use your scissors (ask a grown-up to help you) to pierce holes in the cardboard where you have made dots.

Step 2 Use your needle to pull the thread through one of the holes from the inside of the tube. Thread it through your bell and back through the hole in the tube.

Tie the two ends of thread in a tight knot inside the cardboard tube. Repeat step 2 until you have fixed all the bells to the cardboard.

Step 3 Glue one end of the ribbon just below the bells and wrap it around the tube. Alternate the ribbons to make a stripy pattern.

Step 4 Now shake those Jingle-Jangle Bells **loudly** and softly, just like Elephant!

About Carrie and David

Carrie and David are best known for their hugely successful CBeebies series, **Carrie and David's Popshop**. They have coached Take That, The Saturdays and The Spice Girls and have a top-selling vocal coaching book and DVD. In 2008 they were awarded a BASCA for their lifetime services to the music industry.

Parents to four children, Carrie and David are passionate about getting all children to sing and are keen to encourage adults to feel more confident in teaching their little ones music skills from an early age. The **Jump Up And Join In** series was born as a result of this passion and will help young children learn a set of basic skills and develop a real love of music. As ambassadors for **Sing Up** – a not-for-profit organisation providing the complete singing solution for schools – and judges of the young singers on BBC 1's **Comic Relief Does Glee Club**, Carrie and David believe children everywhere should be given the tools to enjoy, and to feel confident about, practising music in all its shapes and forms.

Thanks for jumping up
and joining in!
Till the next time, bye!